WELCOME TO SWA... ...DOW

HOME OF

BILLY THE BUS

BILLY THE BUS
Copyright © Mark McDaid 2006
Illustrated by Jan Konopka

ISBN 1 84401 714 1

First Published 2006 by
ATHENA PRESS
Queen's House, 2 Holly Road
Twickenham, TW1 4EG
United Kingdom

Printed for Athena Press

BILLY THE BUS

To Cerise
Enjoy Billy
Love
Mark McDaid
x

MARK McDAID

ATHENA PRESS, LONDON

The sign above the door says: 'Welcome to Swan's Meadow Bus Station'.

It's an old station in the heart of Pool Meadow.

It's home to Rollie, the minibus...

...Bendy, the bus who - you guessed it - bends in the middle...

...Twin Top, the double-decker...

...And Billy, the big red London bus, who no longer lives in London, but was sent to the country when there was a shortage of buses – and he hasn't been back since!

Today was just an ordinary day, no different to any other.

The sun was out and the birds were singing and Billy and the gang were ready for duty as normal.

Billy's driver, Ted, came up and patted him on the bonnet and shouted, 'Good morning, Billy!'

Billy honked his horn and changed his sign to say 'Town Centre'.

'Not today, Billy,' said Ted. 'Guess what we've got today, Billy?'

Billy's front grille smiled – he knew. Rollie looked on and he knew. Twin Top honked his horn and Bendy started to rev up his engine because they all knew.

'Yes, that's right, Billy,' said Ted. 'We've got the school run!'

Every bus dreams of days like these!

Ted checked Billy's water and oil and settled into his big black seat, rang his bell and started him up – first time, as always, with no problem. Ted turned the big white steering wheel and Billy proudly moved out of the station ready to take the children to school.

Bendy was on his way as well, snaking his way through the streets, picking up and dropping off all the townsfolk, who were going shopping or going to work.

Bendy was long and bright green, and smartly displayed his bus station badge on both his sides. He was a proud bus, and sometimes he laughed to himself when he took tight corners because he could see his back door in his mirrors.

The station controller, Jack, came up to Twin Top and Rollie, holding his clipboard, and said, 'Nothing for you two at the moment, so I'll check you both over ready for this afternoon's rush.'

Billy arrived at his first stop and he picked up the first of the children.

'Good morning, Billy!' they shouted.

Ted pulled on Billy's chain and he gave out a big, impressive *'DING-DING!'*

After three more stops, Billy was on his way to school.

By this time, Rollie was also out doing the supermarket run, which left Twin Top all alone at the station. Poor old Twin Top – he felt lonely and left out.

'I'm sorry, Twin Top,' said Jack. 'I just don't have anything for you to do today. You're too big for the other runs, but just right for the weekend when there are more runs to do, especially for a double-decker.'

Twin Top was still feeling left out. He did not want to wait till Saturday, because today was Monday and so there were five whole days to go. But what could he do?

Jack had to go to the office so he could hear Ted on the radio.

'BENDY IS STUCK ON A VERY
TIGHT BEND IN TOWN',
SAID TED.
'I'M GOING TO TAKE A LOOK
AND SEE IF I CAN HELP.'

SWAN MEADOW

By this time, Rollie was there as well, and all three buses were now stuck in traffic! Bendy was well and truly stuck. It was his own fault, really, as he had been looking at himself in the mirror and had taken the corner too tightly.

'We'll have to reverse you out, Bendy,' said Ted. Bendy had now been stuck for a while and Billy and Rollie were just as stuck.

Ted called on the radio to Jack: 'WE MUST GET THE CHILDREN AND TOWNSFOLK PICKED UP SOON, JACK, BUT WE CAN'T MOVE!'

Jack looked at Twin Top and shouted, 'Right, it's up to us to save the day, Twin Top. Let's go!'

Twin Top felt important again.

Twin Top went straight to the school and picked up the waiting children right on time.

He made a detour to the supermarket to pick up people there and then on to the railway station to do his last pick-up. He was full.

Twin Top dropped everyone off at the correct stops and went back to the station.

By this time, Billy and the gang were back, including Bendy, who looked on with shame, but got a pat from Jack who said, 'Nice to see you back Bendy… in one piece!' He laughed.

Ted and Jack stood in the middle of the station holding a cup of tea each.

'A toast,' Jack said, 'to Twin Top, because without him we wouldn't have got everybody home safe and sound tonight.'

They both raised their cups and shouted 'Hip hip hooray!' three times.

Billy and Rollie rang their bells and Bendy... well, he was just far too busy looking at himself in his mirrors again!

Will he ever learn? I think not!

THE END

Mark McDaid lives in the Warwickshire market town of Shipston on Stour with his wife Catherine. This is his first short story and was initially written for Robyn, his niece, for her birthday. Watch out for the next adventures of Billy the Bus and his friends.

Printed in Great Britain
by Amazon.co.uk, Ltd.,
Marston Gate.